to the teacher

Pendulum Press is proud to offer the NOW AGE ILLUSTRATED Series to schools throughout the country. This completely new series has been prepared by the finest artists and illustrators from around the world. The script adaptations have been prepared by professional writers and revised by qualified reading consultants.

Implicit in the development of the Series are several assumptions. Within the limits of propriety, anything a child reads and/or wants to read is *per se* an educational tool. Educators have long recognized this and have clamored for materials that incorporate this premise. The sustained popularity of the illustrated format, for example, has been documented, but it has not been fully utilized for educational purposes. Out of this realization, the NOW AGE ILLUSTRATED Series evolved.

In the actual reading process, the illustrated panel encourages and supports the student's desire to read printed words. The combination of words and picture helps the student to a greater understanding of the subject; and understanding, that comes from reading, creates the desire for more reading.

The final assumption is that reading as an end in itself is self-defeating. Children are motivated to read material that satisfies their quest for knowledge and understanding of their world. In this series, they are exposed to some of the greatest stories, authors, and characters in the English language. The Series will stimulate their desire to read the original edition when their reading skills are sufficiently developed. More importantly, reading books in the NOW AGE ILLUSTRATED Series will help students establish a mental "pegboard" of information—images, names, and concepts—to which they are exposed. Let's assume, for example, that a child sees a television commercial which features Huck Finn in some way. If he has read the NOW AGE Huck Finn, the TV reference has meaning for him which gives the child a surge of satisfaction and accomplishment.

After using the NOW AGE ILLUSTRATED editions, we know that you will share our enthusiasm about the series and its concept.

—The Editors

The Hound
of the Baskervilles

Sir Arthur Conan Doyle

ILLUSTRATED

Pendulum Press, Inc.

West Haven, Connecticut

ISBN 0-88301-093-3 Complete Set
0-88301 264-2 This Volume

Library of Congress Catalog Card Number 77-79437

Published by
Pendulum Press, Inc.
An Academic Industries, Inc. Company
The Academic Building
Saw Mill Road
West Haven, Connecticut 06516

Printed in the United States of America

about the author

Sir Arthur Conan Doyle, an English novelist, was born in 1859 and knighted in 1902. He was educated at Stonyhurst College in Germany and at Edinburgh University. He received an M.B. in 1881 and M.D. in 1885. He was a practicing physician in Southsea, England prior to his career as an author.

In 1891 he attained immense popularity for *The Great Adventures of Sherlock Holmes.* These stories follow the capers of Sherlock Holmes who detected crime and untangled mysteries with an uncanny talent. *The Hound of the Baskervilles* is probably this character's most famous case. Set on the moors of northern England, it combines the atmosphere of the strange and supernatural with the suspense of skilled detective work.

Although his stories were often imitated, none were as successful as the Sherlock Holmes stories. In his later years, Doyle was a convinced spiritualist, and he wrote and lectured on spiritualism.

Sir Arthur
Conan Doyle

The Hound
Of The
Baskervilles

Adapted by
JOHN NORWOOD FAGO

Illustrated by
E. R. CRUZ

a
VINCENT FAGO
production

Sir Henry
Baskerville

Mr. Jack Stapleton

Sherlock
Holmes

Dr. Watson

Beryl Stapleton

Dr. Mortimer

My name is Dr. Watson and I am a close friend of Sherlock Holmes, the well-known detective.

Early one morning, I found Mr. Holmes seated at the break-fast table in our London flat. *

*apartment

My eye was caught by a walking stick left by a visitor who had missed us the evening before.

Well, Watson, what do you make of it?

I see that this cane was given to a Dr. James Mortimer from his friends of the C.C.H., 1884.

He is, no doubt, a country doctor who does his visiting on foot. And the "friends of the C.C.H." are members of a hunt club he has helped.

Really, Watson, you outdo yourself.

I must admit that these words gave me great pleasure. With some self-importance I asked:

Have I missed anything, Holmes?

As a matter of fact, you have, Watson. But I am glad. In finding your mistakes, I am often led to the truth. The man is certainly a country doctor who walks a great deal.

Note that the date is just five years ago. A good city doctor is not likely to move to the country.

Dr. Mortimer seems to be a young fellow, under thirty, friendly, absent-minded, and the owner of a small dog.

Yes, by Jove! It is a curly-haired spaniel!*

My dear fellow, how can you possibly be so sure of that?

*a small hunting dog

For the simple reason that I see the dog waiting on our front doorstep. And I now hear his master's knock on our door.

KNOCK KNOCK

Dr. Mortimer wore a clean but rumpled suit. It made him look warm and friendly, as Holmes had guessed earlier. As he came in, the first thing he saw was his walking stick.

And now, Dr. James Mortimer . . .

I am so very glad. I would not lose this stick for the world!

I know that I speak to a man with a quick mind.

I read a little science, Mr. Holmes.

Holmes was silent, but his eyes showed me the interest he had in our visitor.

I come to you because I have a problem which I cannot solve alone.

This family paper was put into my care by Sir Charles Baskerville. As you might know, he died suddenly three months ago.

It is a legend* about the Baskerville family. I would like to read it to you.

"Learn from this story not to fear the evil that some of our family has done in the past, but to be more careful in the future. This may protect us from the curse** that has followed our family.

*n old story
*an evil wish that often brings harm

The story of the Hound of the Baskervilles goes back many years to Hugo Baskerville, a cruel man who once lived in the old manor house.

One evening he went with some wicked men and kidnapped the daughter of a farmer who lived nearby. Her father and brothers were away at the time.

The girl was locked in an upper room while Hugo and his friends sat down to drink the night away.

Driven by fear, the girl escaped and ran home across the fields.

When Hugo left his guests to visit the girl, he discovered her escape. Flying into a rage, he called for his dogs.

Crying aloud that he would give his soul to the devil if he could catch the girl, he rode off into the darkness.

When Hugo's friends caught up with him, they found his hounds huddled together looking down a narrow valley.

Only three men dared enter. By the light of the moon they saw the girl lying dead. Nearby lay the body of Hugo, with a giant black hound tearing at his throat.

The beast was more frightening than anything they had ever seen. Screaming, they turned and ran back across the moor. *

swampy field

Now this from a Devon County newspaper of this year. "The recent death of Sir Charles Baskerville has cast a gloom over the county."

"He was kind and generous. He had great plans for improving the lives of the people in Devonshire."

"On March 14, Sir Charles had gone for his usual walk in the garden. When he did not return, his butler, Barrymore, went looking for him.

Barrymore found the body of Sir Charles in the garden. There were no signs of a struggle, but his face was twisted out of shape by fear."

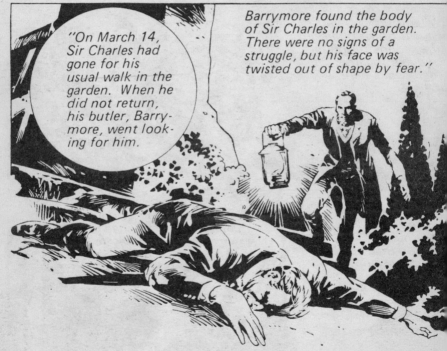

A doctor's report found that Sir Charles' death was caused by heart disease. It was hoped that this would end the stories people were telling about the way he died.

These are the public facts. Now give me the private ones!

In the months before his death, it had become plain to me that Sir Charles was close to the breaking point. He had taken the family legend to heart.

His fear was so great that nothing could draw him out upon the moors at night.

He asked me if, on my medical calls at night, I had ever seen a strange creature or heard the baying* of a hound.

One day as I arrived at Baskerville Hall, Sir Charles greeted me at the door. His face suddenly froze in horror, and I turned around in time to see what seemed to be a large black calf.

*the barking sound of hunting dogs

And on the night of Sir Charles' death, I discovered footprints near his body.

A man's or a woman's?

Mr. Holmes, they were the footprints of a giant hound!

The gate was the only entrance to the garden from the moor. A study of the ground showed that Sir Charles had stood there for five or ten minutes.

How do you know that?

Because the ash had twice dropped from his cigar.

Very good! This is a man after our own hearts!

Others have seen a creature upon the moor that sounds like the Baskerville hound.

All tell the same story of a dreadful sight like the animal of the legend. None but a fool will cross the moor at night!

My problem now is to meet Sir Charles' only relative, who is coming from Canada. He will be at Waterloo Station in only fifty minutes. But I am afraid to take him to Baskerville Hall!

I think you should take a cab and meet him at Waterloo Station. Say nothing about this until we meet again. Please return tomorrow morning and bring him with you.

Holmes fell into deep thought, and I left him alone for the rest of the day.

When I returned that evening, I feared a fire had broken out. Smoke filled the room.

Caught cold, Watson?

No, it's this awful smoke!

After you left I sent for these maps of the moor. My spirit has traveled it all day.

But my body, while staying behind in this armchair, has used up two pots of coffee and a large amount of tobacco.

What have you found out?

Simply that an old man, known to be in poor health, waited on a damp evening by a gate . . .

But for whom did he wait, and why? But now I am going to play my violin and stop all thought of this until morning.

The next day . . .

Pleased to meet you, Mr. Holmes! I understand that you solve puzzles. I've had one this morning.

I would like to hear about it!

I've spent my life in the United States and Canada. But I hope that having one new boot disappear from my hotel room is not common here.

That is strange! Have you noticed anyone watching or following you?

No, but I did receive a strange letter at my hotel. The message was formed by words cut from a newspaper and pasted down. It read . . .

"If you value your life, keep away from the moor." But why should anyone watch or follow me?

We shall see. Now, while I look at the letter, I think Dr. Mortimer should tell Sir Henry the Baskerville story.

This is too much for a man to understand at one time. Mr. Holmes, won't you and Dr. Watson come later for lunch at my hotel?

Of course!

So our visitors left. Holmes suddenly changed from a dreamer to a man of action.

Your hat and boots, Watson, quick! There's not a moment to lose!

We followed them into Oxford Street and then down into Regent Street.

There's our man, Watson! Quick! Come along! We'll have a good look at him!

Suddenly I saw a man with a bushy black beard looking at us from the cab window. He screamed to the driver and the cab moved off down Regent Street.

Too bad that in our haste we have let ourselves be seen and lost our man!

We will stop at an art gallery and fill in the time till we are due at Sir Henry's hotel.

For two hours we spoke only of paintings.

But when we arrived at Sir Henry's room at the hotel . . .

I don't understand the servants here. Last night they took one of my new brown boots, and now it's one of my old black ones!

It's the strangest thing that ever happened to me!

This case of yours is very strange. But we now hold several threads in our hands. The odds are that one of them will guide us to the truth.

At lunch Holmes asked Sir Henry about his plans.

No man on earth can prevent me from going to my family home.

Quite so, Sir Henry, but you must not stay there alone!

Who do you think should stay with me?

If Watson would go, there could be no better man at your side.

I would be happy to do so.

We decided to leave the next Saturday for Baskerville Hall.

Nothing is more interesting than a difficult case! I wish you good luck at Baskerville Hall!

Let me hear from you often. Report whatever you find out.

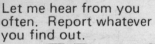

Remember the warning in the family legend, Sir Henry. Stay off the moor at night!

The trip was swift and pleasant. But I was surprised to see two soldiers at the station.

At each turn of the road, Sir Henry gave a gasp of joy. To his eyes, all seemed beautiful. But then Dr. Mortimer saw another soldier.

What's this all about, Perkins?

A man has escaped from Princetown jail, sir. Soldiers are looking for him everywhere. It's Selden, the Notting Hill killer!

I remembered the case. It had been a bloody one. A cold wind blew over us, and even Sir Henry fell silent.

The house was a ruin. But facing it was a new hall, half-built. It had been the work of Sir Charles.

No wonder my uncle felt fearful in such a place! I'll have electric lamps leading to the front door within six months!

Welcome to Baskerville Hall!

The butler Barrymore and his wife greeted us.

With rows of flaming torches and a large family eating dinner, the old dining room might once have been a cheerful place. But tonight it seemed very dark indeed.

My word, but it's a gloomy place!

It's late now, and we're tired. Things may look brighter in the morning.

I tossed and turned and slept poorly that night. Once I thought I heard the sound of a woman sobbing . . .

. . . but though I tried to listen, I heard nothing but the chiming of a clock and the wind outside.

The beauty of the next morning came as a welcome change.

Did you hear a woman crying last night?

I thought I heard something, but then I decided it was only a dream.

At breakfast Sir Henry asked Barrymore if he knew anything about a crying woman.

No sir, I don't. It was not my wife.

But when I met Mrs. Barrymore after breakfast, I could see that her eyes were red from crying.

Later I went for a walk upon the moor. Soon I came upon one of the few people who lived near Baskerville Hall.

Excuse me, sir. I am Stapleton of Merripit House.

I guessed that from your net and box. Dr. Mortimer told me that you study animals. I am Dr. Watson.

Stapleton invited me to visit Merripit House and meet his sister. I gladly accepted. But as I followed him along the moor, I heard a strange sound.

What's that?

A queer place, the moor.

A long, low moan, very sad, swept over the moor.

But what is it?

They say it's the Hound of the Baskervilles. I've heard it before, but never so loud.

We kept walking and Stapleton told me of the country's forgotten folk.

Prehistoric* men once lived here on the moor.

*He also told me about Grimpen Mire** and gave me a warning.*

A false step there means death! But that's where the rare plants and butterflies are if you know what you're doing Look! It's a Cyclopides!***

A small fly or moth had fluttered across our path. In a moment, Stapleton was after it.

I watched Stapleton run off. Then, hearing the sound of steps, I turned to see a woman near me upon the path.

*before history was written down
**a place on the moor where there was deep, soft mud
***a kind of moth

You must get away from this place!

But I've only just come!

Hush! My brother is coming!

Hello, Beryl. I was chasing a Cyclopides. They are very rare this late in autumn, you know.

Yes, I was just telling Sir Henry that it is rather late to see the true beauties of the moor.

But I am not Sir Henry! I am his friend. My name is Dr. Watson.

Shall we go along now and see Merripit House?

I could not help but wonder what might have brought this man and woman to live here.

I had a school once, but we had to close it. I'm happy here with my work.

Isn't it dull for your sister?

No, I am never bored. We have our books and studies. But I miss Sir Charles greatly.

Soon I started home along the path I had used before. It surprised me to find Beryl Stapleton waiting to speak to me.

She had taken a short cut in order to catch up with me. She begged me to take Sir Henry away. I asked her why she didn't want her brother to know about her wish.

My brother wants the Hall lived in for the good of the poor people on the moor. My wish would make him angry.

When she left me, was filled with a great sense of fear.

A little later, Stapleton stopped in at Baskerville Hall to meet Sir Henry. He invited us to dinner the next evening.

The following morning he took us to the spot where the legend of Hugo Baskerville had started.

Our dinner with the Stapletons went well. It was also plain that Sir Henry was attracted to Miss Stapleton. The feeling seemed to be returned.

I could not help but make a note of it in my regular report to Holmes.

Though they seem to like one another, I do not think that Stapleton wants it to turn into love. He would certainly lead her a lonely life without her. But it seems selfish of him to stand in the way of such a good marriage.

That evening I woke up in the middle of the night. Someone was walking quietly past my door.

His outline and height told me it was Barrymore. There was something secret about the way he moved.

I followed him to a bare room at the end of the hall.

He stood for a moment beside a window and then blew out his candle. I hurried back to my room.

In the morning before breakfast I visited the room. I could see that it faced the moor. Barrymore had been giving a signal to someone standing out there!

When I spoke of this to Sir Henry, he was not surprised.

Yes. Several times I have heard steps at that hour.

I wonder if i happens ever night!

I think we should get to the bottom of this!

Good! We'll wait in my room tonight until he passes.

Later that morning Sir Henry prepared to take a walk upon the moor.

Are you coming Watson?

You know my orders from Holmes. You must not go out alone upon the moor!

My dear Watson, I am going out to meet Miss Stapleton! I must have some time alone with her.

To spy upon a friend is not easy. Still, I could not let something happen to Sir Henry because I did not do my job.

Suddenly I saw that I was not the only one watching them.

There was a short argument be-fore Stapleton led his sister away. Sir Henry was angry because he could not see Miss Stapleton alone.

It puzzles me, Watson! I still feel she was made for me!

I asked her to marry me! Before she could answer, that brother of hers came down like a madman!

It does seem strange.

Much to our surprise, we received a visit from Stapleton that very afternoon. He wanted to have a private talk with Sir Henry.

He said he was sorry and that the thought of his sister's leaving him had clouded his reason.

He said he wanted more time to get used to the idea. He asked me to be only her friend for the next three months. Then he invited us for dinner the next Friday.

And so we turned to the mystery of Barry-more's late-night walks.

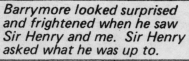

Barrymore looked surprised and frightened when he saw Sir Henry and me. Sir Henry asked what he was up to.

Nothing, sir! Just checking the windows!

Look here, Barrymore, we want the truth!

Please, sir! It's not my secret to tell!

Your family has lived with mine for many years, and now you have some dark plot against me!

No sir. It is not against you! And it is all my doing!

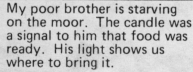

My poor brother is starving on the moor. The candle was a signal to him that food was ready. His light shows us where to bring it.

You mean your brother is the escaped killer?

It's true, sir, every word of it!

Well I can't blame you for standing by your wife. We'll talk more about this in the morning.

We set out across the moor. We thought it was our duty to help put this poor madman back where he could do no more harm.

Suddenly there rose that strange cry I had heard once before.

Can there be any truth to these stories?

My God, what's that, Watson?

They say it's the cry of the Hound of the Baskervilles!

Shall we turn back?

No, by thunder! We'll see it through, even if all the devils are loose upon the moor!

And so we went on.

But before we could call to the man we saw, he spotted us and ran.

Though a lucky shot might have stopped him, I had brought my gun only for self-defense. I would not shoot an unarmed man.

We chased him, but quickly saw we had no chance of catching him.

Walking home, something strange happened. I saw the figure of another man who had been watching us.

He was tall and thin. As I turned to touch Sir Henry's arm, he was gone.

The following morning there was a small scene after breakfast.

I didn't think you gentlemen would do anything about our secret!

The man is a public danger! Think of the Stapletons in their lonely house!

I give my word he'll be gone in a few days!

What do you say, Watson?

If he were out of the country, it would save the taxpayers some money!

I think we're aiding a crime, but I don't feel we should give him up.

You've been kind to us, sir. Now I will tell you why Sir Charles was at the moor gate on the night of his death!

We found the burned remains of a letter in Sir Charles' study. We were still able to make something out.

Barrymore read us a message from a scrap of burned paper. It was in a lady's handwriting and asked Sir Charles to meet her at the moor gate at ten o'clock.

She also asked him to burn the letter. She signed it L. L. It had been mailed from Coombe Tracy. *

I said nothing of this before because I did not want to harm my master's good name.

I'll tell Holmes right away. This news may bring him down.

I went to my room and wrote to Holmes. I felt sure that this news was important.

*a nearby town

It rained all the next day. I thought of Selden on the cold moor. Poor devil! Whatever his crimes, he was suffering now!

On my way home I took a ride with Dr. Mortimer. I asked him if he knew a woman in the area whose initials were L. L.

H'mmmm. Well, there is Laura Lyons, but she lives over in Coombe Tracy.

Since she married against her father's wishes, he would not help her.

But what of that figure seen against the moon, that person who had watched us?

In the evening I put on my raincoat and walked far out on the moor. I found no trace of that lonely man I had seen two nights before.

Who is she?

Old Frankland, who lives on the moor, is her father. She married an artist named Lyons, who went away and left her alone.

Mortimer also said that Stapleton and Sir Charles had helped set the woman up in a typewriting business. They wanted to help her earn an honest living.

And that evening Barrymore gave me some more news. He said that he had not heard from Selden and that the food left for him was gone. But he added that it might have been taken by the other stranger!

What? You know about the other man?

Selden had told Barrymore that the other man lived in the old stone huts on the moor. Food was brought to him by a child.

Very good! We will talk more of this later.

With these two pieces of news, I felt sure that more was soon to be learned.

The following morning after sharing the news with Sir Henry, I went to pay a visit to Mrs. Lyons.

Did you ever write Sir Charles, asking him to meet you?

Really, sir. This is a strange question!

I am sorry, but I must ask it again.

Well, then, I did no such thing!

Surely you are wrong. I quote, "Please, if you are a gentleman, burn this letter . . ."

Is there no such thing as a gentleman?

Do not judge Sir Charles. Sometimes a letter may still be read even after it is burned.

Mrs. Lyons said that she wrote to Sir Charles because she needed money to divorce her cruel husband. But she added that she never went to see him because she received the money from someone else.

Why didn't you write to Sir Charles and tell him this?

I would have done so, but then I read of his death. It was in the paper the next morning.

I felt that part of what she said was true. But the more I thought of her face and manner, the more sure I was that she was holding something back from me.

I had a bit of luck on my way home. As we passed his house, Mr. Frankland called to me.

Dr. Watson! Come in and share a glass of wine.

I sent the driver home so that I could walk back across the moor. I wanted to search the stone huts.

Frankland always seemed to be fighting someone. At that time it was the townspeople and the police. He told me that he knew secrets they would like to have.

Do you know something about the killer they are looking for?

No, but his food is taken to him by a child. I see it every day through my telescope.* Come and look!

Here was luck! Barrymore had said that the other stranger was given food by a boy. I promised Frankland not to tell his secret to anyone.

*a glass which makes things far away seem larger

As quickly as I could, I said goodbye and started off after the boy.

At last my foot was on the doorstep of his hiding place. His secret was very nearly mine.

I moved carefully through the door of the hut. It was empty. So, seating myself in a dark corner, I waited for the return of the man who lived there.

As the sun was setting, I heard footsteps. Taking out my gun, I prepared myself.

It is a lovely evening, my dear Watson. I really think you would like it better outside.

Holmes! Holmes!

Please be careful with that gun!

I was never more glad to see any-one in my whole life!

Or more surprised, eh?

At first I was very happy. But later I felt that I had been tricked.

Then Holmes told me that it was important for him to be in hiding. He had not wanted our enemies to know that he was on the case.

Now when we put our findings to-gether, the case will be almost complete.

But why keep me in the dark and waste all my reports?

At that, Holmes pulled my repor from his pocket. I could see that they had been read carefully. then shared with him the results my visit to Laur Lyons.

There seems to be a strong bond between this woman and Stapleton. However, we will see what happens when she learns of his wife.

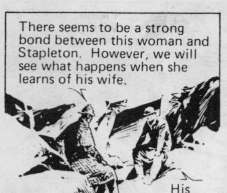

His wife?

Yes, the lady who has passed as Miss Stapleton is really his wife!

Good heavens, Holmes! Are you sure of what you say?

Holmes told me that he had learned about the Stapletons' school from my reports. He then did some studying and came across a few important facts.

He found the story of a school closing that was much like Stapleton's. There had been a crime, and the owner had left with his wife. When he learned that the missing man liked to study insects, he was sure it was Stapleton.

Then he is our enemy? He is the one who followed Sir Henry in London?

Enough for now! The end is drawing near. But Watson, shouldn't you be with Sir Henry?

Good heavens! What is that?

HELP! HELP!
000 - 000 - 000

But just at that moment a human scream burst out of the moor. It turned the blood in my veins to ice. After that came the terrible baying of the Baskerville Hound.

Fool that I was to wait! And Watson, you should never have left him alone! But by heaven, we'll get to the bottom of this yet!

There was no mistaking that odd tweed suit that Sir Henry Baskerville had worn that first morning on Baker Street.

Oh Holmes, I'll never forgive myself!

Watson! A beard! A beard! The man has a beard!

Poor Selden was wearing a suit of Sir Henry's clothes, given to him by Barrymore.

It's clear that the hound was put on the scent by Sir Henry's old boot—the one stolen from the hotel!

But what's this? It's the man himself! Not a word!

It was Stapleton. He seemed startled when he saw us but came ahead.

Why, Dr. Watson, you're the last man I'd expect to see on the moor this time of night. But dear me, what's this? Somebody hurt?

Who . . . who's this?

We told him that it was the man who had escaped from jail. He seemed to have broken his neck in a fall over the rocks.

And what do you think about it, Mr. Sherlock Holmes?

You are quick to know me! I have no answers and will have none since I am due back in London tomorrow. But I am sure that the answer is simple.

Tomorrow? We've been looking forward to your help in throwing some light on these puzzles.

In the clearest way he could, Holmes told Stapleton that a detective needed facts rather than stories to work with. He said that this had been a very strange case.

We covered the body and set off quickly for Baskerville Hall.

I am sorry that he has seen you.

It may drive him to do something more reckless at once.

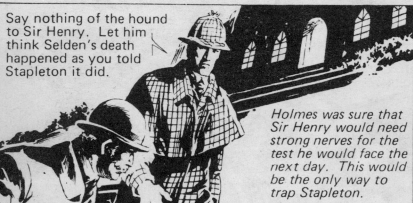

Say nothing of the hound to Sir Henry. Let him think Selden's death happened as you told Stapleton it did.

Holmes was sure that Sir Henry would need strong nerves for the test he would face the next day. This would be the only way to trap Stapleton.

Sir Henry was more pleased than surprised to see Sherlock Holmes.

Welcome, good sir!

Over a late supper we told Sir Henry as much of our story as he needed to know.

It was my job to break the sad news to Barrymore and his wife. He seemed glad that it was over, but she wept for a long time.

To the world Selden had been half animal, half devil. But to her, he would always be her little brother.

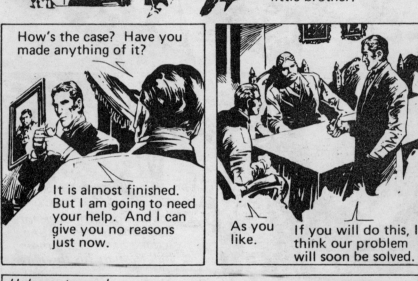

How's the case? Have you made anything of it?

It is almost finished. But I am going to need your help. And I can give you no reasons just now.

As you like.

If you will do this, I think our problem will soon be solved.

Holmes stopped talking suddenly and stared in a strange way at a point beyond the top of my head.

What is it?

Pardon me for staring, but I find these family pictures most interesting!

There's the cause of all this trouble. That is Hugo who started the story of the Baskerville Hound.

Dear me, he seems a quiet enough man, though I see a bit of the devil in those eyes.

Holmes said little more, but I could see how interested he was in the picture of Hugo.

It was not until Sir Henry had gone to bed that he led me back to the dining hall to share his thoughts.

Good heavens! It's Stapleton!

Ha, you see it now! The fellow is a Baskerville, that is sure!

So he plans to be the next heir?*

Exactly! But this picture is our missing link. Tomorrow night he will be in our nets as helpless as one of his own butterflies.

With this, Holmes burst into one of his rare fits of laughter. I have not heard it often, but it has always meant bad luck for someone.

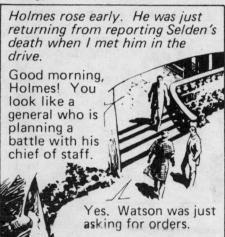

Holmes rose early. He was just returning from reporting Selden's death when I met him in the drive.

Good morning, Holmes! You look like a general who is planning a battle with his chief of staff.

Yes. Watson was just asking for orders.

Very good. You have been invited to dine with the Stapletons tonight?

And so am I!

I am counting on your coming also!

I am sorry, but business calls Watson and me to London. Please tell your friends. We will return soon.

*a person who is left property by someone who has died

I had hoped you would see me through this terrible time!

My dear fellow, you must trust me. You've given me your word that you would do as you were told.

I want you to drive to Merripit House but send the carriage home. Let the Stapletons know that you intend to walk home later.

But this is what you've warned me never to do!

This time you may do it in safety! Remember, you must do just as I say!

Then I will do it.

And no matter what happens as you cross the moor, do not take a single step off the path that is your way home!

And so we said goodbye to our worried friend.

We went to the Coombe Tracy station where Holmes received a telegram.

Telegram

WIRE RECEIVED
COMING DOWN
WITH UNSIGNED
WARRANT
ARRIVE
FIVE-FORTY

LESTRADE

This man is one of the best. We may need him. And now to call on Mrs. Laura Lyons.

His plan was beginning to take shape. He would have Sir Henry tell Stapleton that we had gone, while we would really be close when needed.

This seems to be a case of murder which concerns your friend Mr. Stapleton. It seems also to concern his wife.

His wife? He is not a married man!

Holmes then showed her a photo taken four years ago. While the name was different, the couple were clearly Jack and Beryl Stapleton.

This man offered to marry me if I could divorce my husband!

He lied to me! I never dreamed, when I wrote that letter, that any harm would come to Sir Charles, my dearest friend!

Was the sending of this letter suggested by Stapleton?

He told me what to write!

When you learned of Sir Charles' death, did he make you swear to say nothing?

He frightened me into keeping quiet. He said that I would be in trouble if any of the facts came out.

I expect he gave as his reason the need to get help from Sir Charles for the cost of your divorce.

Yes. But later he said that he could not allow anyone else to help me. At his urging I did not meet Sir Charles.

I thought I knew him. But if he had kept faith with me, I would have always done so with him.

You had him in your power and he knew it. Yet you are still alive. You are very lucky. Good morning, Mrs. Lyons. You will hear from us again.

Our case becomes rounded off! It is very nearly done!

We met Lestrade at the station.

This case is quite like another which took place in Russia. But this one has a few points all its own!

Anything good?

The biggest thing in years. Let's have our dinner. Then we'll give you a breath of pure night air on the moor. Never been there? Ah, well, I don't suppose you'll forget your first visit!

We were about to take our last step in the case, and yet Holmes had said nothing. I could only guess what he was going to do.

Our talk had been cut short because the hired driver had been with us. I was glad when he left and we started out on foot across the moor.

Are you armed, Lestrade?

As long as I have my pants on, I have my hip pocket. As long as I have my hip pocket, I have my gun.

You're mighty quiet about this job, Mr. Holmes. What's the game now?

A waiting game. That's Merripit House ahead, the end of our journe I must ask that y walk on tiptoe ar not talk above a whisper.

Yes, we shall hide here. Watson you creep forward and see what they're doing. But for heaven's sake, don't let them know that they're being watched!

I tiptoed down the path to a low wall that circled the front yard.

Stapleton talked loudly, but Sir Henry looked pale. Perhaps the thought of his lonely walk across the moor was lying heavy upon his thoughts.

As I watched, Stapleton came outside and went to another building in the yard. Some strange noises came from inside the building. He then returned to the house.

You say, Watson, that the lady is not there?

Yes, and it does seem odd!

Suddenly we saw that a thick white fog from the Grimpen Mire was slowly coming toward us.

It's moving this way.

Our success, and even his life, depend upon his coming out before the fog covers this path.

Every minute the white mass drifted closer to the house.

Thank goodness! I think I hear him!

Sir Henry passed quite close to us. As he walked, he kept looking over his shoulder, like a man who is afraid.

Suddenly, there came a series of light tapping sounds from somewhere in the fog between us and the house.

Look out! It's coming!

Never could anything more terrible appear than that dark form which broke upon us out of the fog.

So stunned were we by the sight that we allowed it to pass before we realized it.

Then Holmes and I turned and fired together. The creature gave a terrible howl which blew our fears to the wind. He was real, not a ghost!

What in heaven's name was it?

It's dead, whatever it is! We've laid the family ghost to rest once and for all!

Sir Henry had been badly frightened by his meeting with the hound. He would need a long vacation to forget what had happened to him.

Even in death the huge jaws of the hound seemed to be dripping with flame!

Is it phosphorus?*

Very cleverly done!

Leaving Sir Henry, we rushed to the house to search for Stapleton. Upstairs we found that one of the bedroom doors was locked.

*a substance that shines in the dark

Holmes smashed the lock. But when we burst into the room, we were faced with a strange sight.

Is Sir Henry safe? Stapleton tied me up when I told him I would no longer do what he wanted!

Yes, madam. But where is your husband? If you have ever helped him in his evil plans, help us now and make up for it!

There is an old tin mine in the middle of Grimpen Mire. It was there he kept the hound and stored his supplies.

words to know

legend	prehistoric	flat
curse	telescope	baying
moor	heir	phosphorus

questions

1. Who was Dr. James Mortimer? What role did he play in this mystery story?

2. Why did Sir Henry Baskerville come to England from Canada? What strange things happened to him at his hotel the day after he arrived?

3. Why did Dr. Watson go with Sir Henry to Baskerville Hall?

4. Who were the Stapletons? What had Mr. Stapleton been trying to do throughout the story? Why?

5. Besides Selden, an escaped convict, someone else was living in a cave on the moors. Who was he, and what was he doing there?

6. Who was Laura Lyons? What role did she play in the story?

7. At the very end, the mystery of the hound of the Baskervilles becomes clear. Was the hound that killed Sir Hugo the same animal that killed Sir Charles and attacked Sir Henry? How do you know?

8. When the story is over, Stapleton is missing. What do you think happened to him? Why?